MOUSE

LINNEA RILEY

MESS

SCHOLASTIC INC.
New York Toronto London Auckland Sydney

This book was originally published in hardcover by
The Blue Sky Press in 1997.

ISBN 0-590-10050-5

40 39 38 37   16 17 18 19/0

Printed in the United States of America   08

Design by Linnea Riley and Kathleen Westray
First Scholastic paperback printing, October 1998

For my dad who loves…

Hush, hush, a little mouse

is sound asleep inside his house.

On the stairs, the sound of feet!

Mouse is up. It's time to eat!

Crunch-crunch, he wants a cracker.

Munch-munch, a cookie snacker.

Crackle-sweep, he rakes corn flakes

and jumps into the pile he makes.

Sniff-sniff, milk and cheese.

Mouse would like a taste of these.

Splish-splash, the milk spills out.

Food is scattered all about.

Sticky-gooey, jam to spread

with peanut butter smeared on bread.

Tipping, slipping, sugar falls.

Pour and pat, make castle walls.

Olives, pickles, catsup—fun!

Pop the tops off, one by one!

Mouse steps back. He looks around.

He can't believe the mess he's found.

"Who made this awful mess?" asks Mouse.

"These   people need to clean their house!"

Gurgle, bubble, water flows,

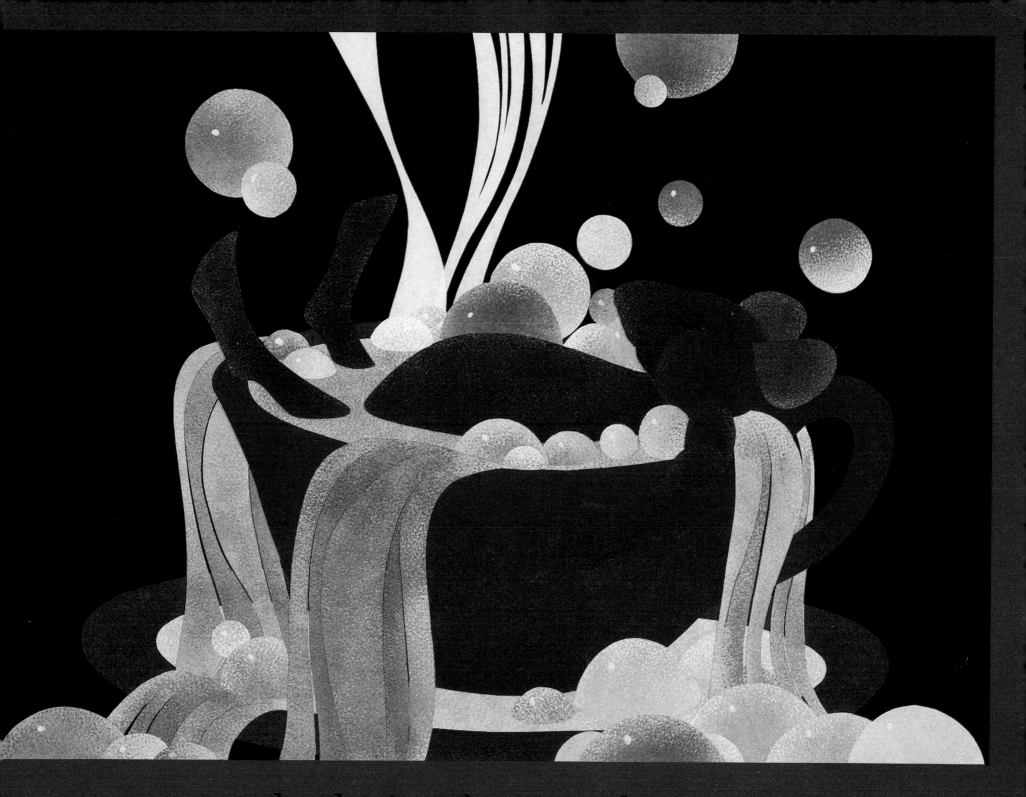

soaks the jam between his toes.

Now that Mouse is clean and fed,

he leaves the mess and goes...

to bed!